SUKI

Silver Anniversary Edition

Suki and the Invisible Peacock
Suki and the Old Umbrella
Suki and the Magic Sand Dollar
Suki and the Wonder Star

Also by Joyce Blackburn

Sir Wilfred Grenfell: Doctor and Explorer

Theodore Roosevelt: Statesman and Naturalist

John Adams: Farmer from Braintree;
Champion of Independence

Martha Berry: A Woman of Courageous Spirit
and Bold Dreams

James Edward Oglethorpe

George Wythe of Williamsburg: Teacher of Jefferson
and Signer of the Declaration of Independence

The Earth Is the Lord's?

Roads to Reality

A Book of Praises

The Bloody Summer of 1742:
A Colonial Boy's Journal

Phoebe's Secret Diary:
Daily Life and First Romance
of a Colonial Girl, 1742

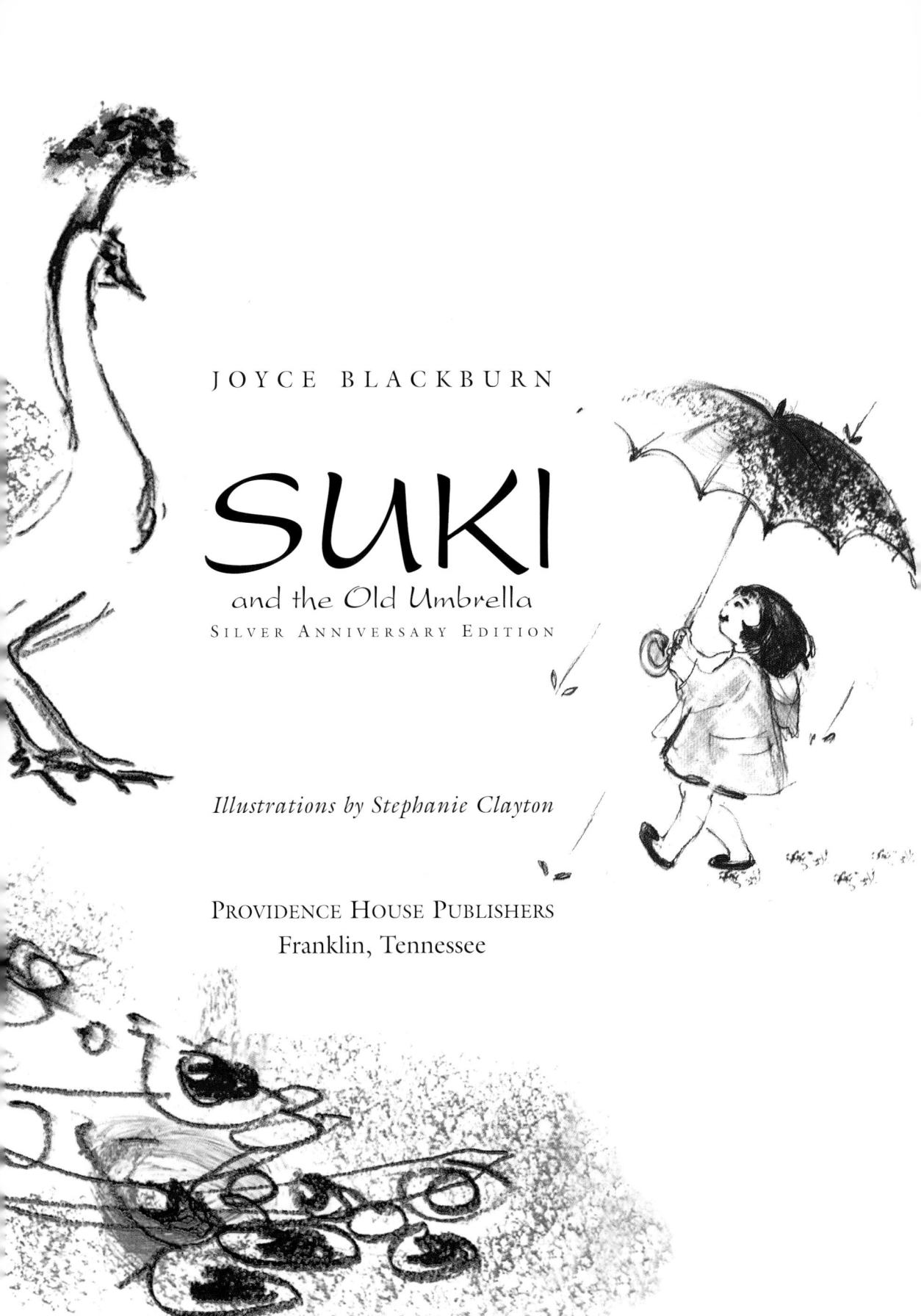

JOYCE BLACKBURN

SUKI
and the Old Umbrella
SILVER ANNIVERSARY EDITION

Illustrations by Stephanie Clayton

PROVIDENCE HOUSE PUBLISHERS
Franklin, Tennessee

First edition 1966. Second edition 1996
Printed in the United States of America

00   99   98   97   96   5   4   3   2   1

Library of Congress Cataloging-in-Publication Data

Blackburn, Joyce.
    Suki and the old umbrella / Joyce Blackburn ; illustrations by
Stephanie Clayton. — 2nd ed.
        p.   cm.
    Summary: Suki's conscience is troubled when she "borrows" a
friend's umbrella.
    ISBN 1–881576–71–X
    [1. Umbrellas and parasols—Fiction. 2. Friendship—Fiction.
3. Rain and rainfall—Fiction. 4. Imaginary playmates—Fiction.
5. Peacocks—Fiction. 6. Japanese Americans—Fiction.]
I. Clayton, Stephanie, ill. II. Title.
PZ7.B53223Suk   1996
[Fic]—dc20
                                                                96–14846
                                                                    CIP
                                                                    AC

Cover design by Schwalb Creative Communications Inc.

PROVIDENCE HOUSE PUBLISHERS
238 Seaboard Lane • Franklin, Tennessee 37067 • 800-321-5692

1

A clap of thunder made Suki cover her ears with her hands. She pretended it scared her. The sound was big and close. But she really liked it, and she could not imagine a spring rain without it.

Once, Daddy had told her a story about an emperor's son who captured the thunder one day. When it rumbled into the palace garden, the prince caught it under his tea bowl and would not let it out until it promised never to return to his kingdom again.

"Can you imagine a storm without thunder, Suki?" Daddy had asked.

Suki tried to imagine.

"No, Daddy. I like it."

After that, when Suki heard thunder, she would say, "Thunder, I like you."

That was why she could not understand her best friend this golden spring evening. Best Friend was an Invisible Peacock who lived in the Paradise tree outside Suki's window. Usually they talked and laughed together. But not this time.

"What *is* the matter with you, Best Friend?" Suki asked, leaning out the window. "You haven't said a word. All you do is cluck, cluck, cluck."

The Invisible Peacock inched back and forth nervously along the limb of the Paradise tree.

"All you have done all day is cluck, cluck, cluck. Why? Why won't you tell me?"

Best Friend gave Suki a gloomy look and said, "Can I help it if I'm a weather prophet?"

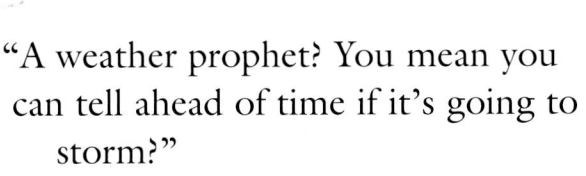

"A weather prophet? You mean you can tell ahead of time if it's going to storm?"

"Yes, Suki, I can." Best Friend sounded miserable.

"But that's fun," Suki cried. "Now you can tell me if it is going to rain or if the thunder is only playing."

"Oh, it's going to rain all right. That's the trouble!"

"What do you mean—trouble?"

"Rain. I hate it. I hate rain. I hate to get wet. All peacocks hate to get wet."

Suki couldn't imagine that anymore than she could imagine storms without thunder. She liked rain. She hoped it would rain all night—and tomorrow. Then she could walk to school in the rain, and maybe she would get wet, a little.

"I think it's fun to get wet, Best Friend. Why don't you think so?"

The Invisible Peacock looked far away and said, "Because two of my baby sisters died in the rainy season. Young peacocks often do."

Before Suki could think of something to say, it thundered again, and the rain began to fall in enormous drops that splashed on her hands and nose. She frowned. How could anything that made Best Friend sad, be so much fun for her?

2

"Don't forget your raincoat, Suki," Mother said at breakfast next morning. "It's raining cats and dogs!"

What a silly thing to say, Suki thought. *Anyone can see it's raining rain—not cats and dogs.*

"The water is up to the curb," Daddy said. "Better wear your boots too."

Boots! Daddy knows I hate boots. They squeeze my feet.

"The last time it rained Suki walked in the puddles, Daddy—on purpose," said Yuri.

Just because you're my older sister you don't have to tell him everything I do. Suki could think anything she wanted to herself and it was all right.

"And she got her head wet and caught a cold," said Mari, her other sister.

Whatever she does is all right. But I'm the "baby" in this family. I can't do anything!

Suki thought plenty, but she did not say a word as she put on her yellow raincoat and buckled it up to her chin. Daddy handed Suki her boots from the hall closet, and Mother snapped the hood to the collar of the raincoat.

They certainly don't mean for me to enjoy this rain. That was what Suki thought as she slammed the door of her daddy's gift shop behind her.

Even Best Friend is trying to spoil the rain for me by staying home. This is the first time since we met he hasn't walked to school with me. Just because he's sad, I'm not going to be sad. He's sad. Too bad.

She made up a little tune to go with the words—

He's sad.
Too bad.

She wished she could just walk around in the rain and listen to the tires of the big mail trucks s-s-sss on the wet pavement. Her boots made a smaller sound—S-L-A-P—S-L-A-P.

At the corner of Clark Street and Wrightwood Avenue, people waited for the bus, their umbrellas bobbing and bumping. She walked around them and came to the back door of Riggs' Bakery. Sometimes she stood there a minute to sniff the tantalizing yeasty odor from the ovens. This morning the baker saw her and called out, "Good weather for ducks, huh, Suki?"

She laughed at him balancing a tray of doughnuts on his head. But as she walked on she thought, *What does he want me to say—q-u-a-c-k?*

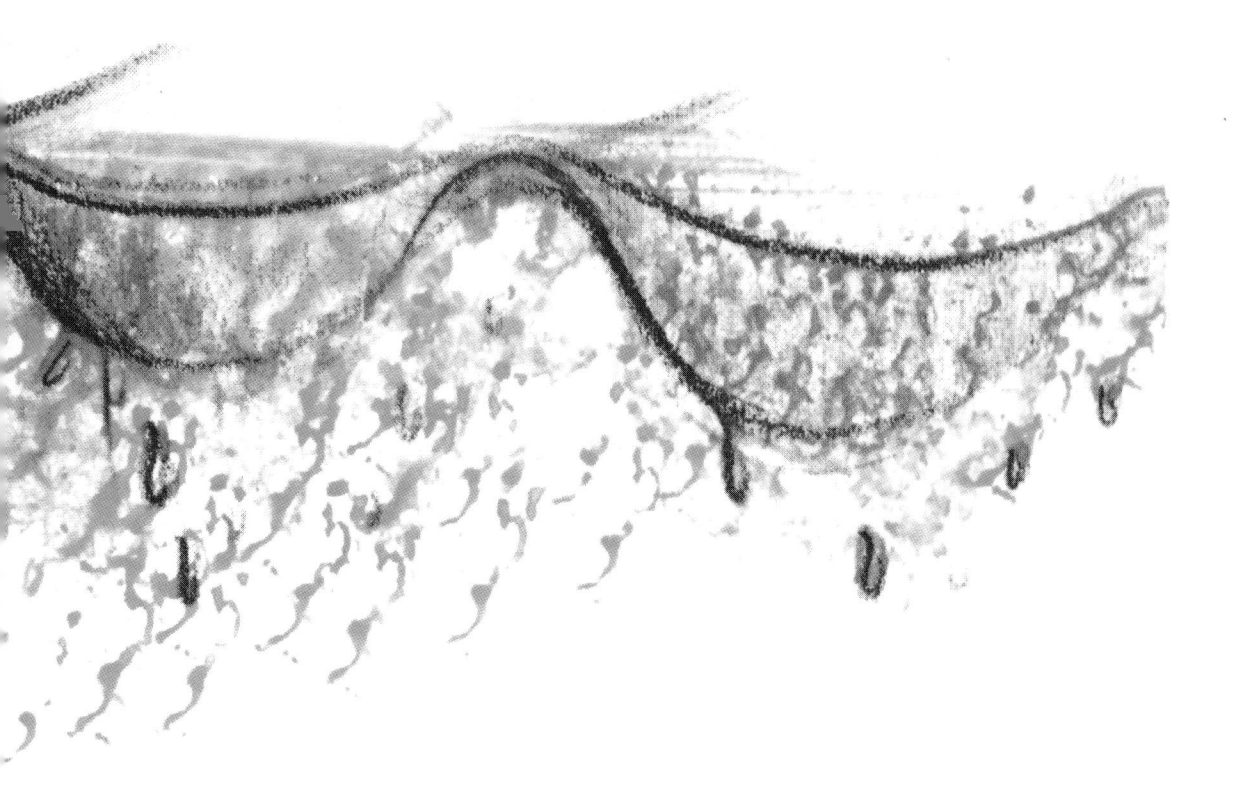

Other children on their way to school were running. She was not going to hurry. The school was still half a block away. She walked under the awning of the Swedish Singing Club.

The awning arched from over the front doors all the way to the curb. Suki stood under one edge where the most water poured off of it. She shut her eyes tightly. She held her breath.

This is like standing under a waterfall!

When she pushed through the shiny wall of water it blinded her for a moment. Her eyelashes were stuck together, and she swallowed a bucketful.

Coughing and spitting and squinting as though a big wave had swept over her, Suki pretended to swim the rest of the way to school.

She shook the yellow raincoat and hung it in her basement locker. She pulled off her boots. Her feet were soaked, and her socks, and the hem of her dress—right in front.

Near the stairway leading from the basement to the first floor, the janitor of the Louisa May Alcott School had an office. Always before the door to it had been closed, and on its frosted glass was lettered in black:

PRIVATE.

This morning the door was open.

It can't hurt to take a peek, Suki thought.

Mr. Mainz, the janitor, was not there, but he had been. On his rolltop desk was a stack of new lightbulbs in their cartons; beside his chair stood a squeegee mop; along one wall supplies crowded the shelves and barrels brimmed with wastepaper.

Just inside the door was an old hall tree, and from one of its brass hooks dangled an umbrella. There was not room for one more thing.

Suki glanced around quickly. Then she backed out of the tiny office, dashed up the stairs to the first floor, and dropped puffing into her seat as the tardy bell began to jangle.

3

On Wednesdays, the first class was Art. Suki liked Art, but the teacher, Miss Kelly, was always saying, "You make lovely use of color, Suki, but your drawing is careless."

The English teacher had said, "You make good sentences, Suki, but your handwriting is careless."

This time I'll be careful, Suki thought as Miss Kelly held up a large conch shell for the class to see.

"This shell will be our subject today," the teacher said. "In your mind's eye you may see it on a beach, on the bottom of the ocean, on a shelf in a store, or on the coffee table at home—any number of places. That's for you to decide."

Suki drew the conch shell with a light brown crayon, leaving some areas white to show its rough surface. The flared-out lip of the shell she colored a rosy pink which faded into pale pink at the edge. Then a funny thing happened. Instead of her mind's eye seeing the shell on a beach or on a shelf or in the water, it seemed to be floating—floating through the air with an umbrella over it!

The umbrella was red—not bright fire-engine red—a rich bing-cherry red, with silver tips, ribs and handle. It was not an ordinary handle at all; it was shaped into a delicate curve as is a swan's neck. In fact, a swan's neck and head were engraved on it with such delicacy and skill that it looked real.

That's the umbrella I saw in Mr. Mainz's office, Suki thought with a start. *It's the prettiest umbrella I have ever seen—not heavy and clumsy like Daddy's—it's the right size for me. Exactly the right size. And the color—I do love the color. It's the color of my new shoes. It matches my new shoes. And that silver swan's head—the eyes and bill and downy neck. . . .*

Suki could feel the lovely shape of it in her hand. It would just fit her hand, she was sure of it.

"In five minutes the bell will ring," Miss Kelly said. "Then you must turn in your pictures and put away your materials."

Suki scarcely heard the teacher for thinking about the umbrella. . . . *If I had an umbrella like the one hanging in Mr. Mainz's office, maybe Best Friend would walk under it with me to school instead of staying home. He doesn't mind getting his feet wet . . . it's the rain on his feathers, especially the fine ones on his head and breast, that makes him so uncomfortable. An umbrella would keep both of us dry . . . on top, at least.*

Suki handed in her picture and went skipping to the next class.

4

The bell rang promptly at 12:00 noon, and all of the girls and boys who went home for lunch scrambled for their raincoats. If possible, it was raining harder than it had rained at 9:00. Suki didn't push with the others; she took her time and walked slowly past Mr. Mainz's office.

The door was still open. Mr. Mainz was not there. The rest of the way to her locker Suki wondered where he could be. She put on her raincoat, hood, and boots, and as though a magnet were tugging at her, retraced her steps to the door of Mr. Mainz's tiny office.

He always smiles at me when we meet, Suki thought. *He always smiles at me and says, "How is the little meisje with the dancing feet?"*

If he were here at this moment, Suki thought, *I would say, "Mr. Mainz, may I please borrow your umbrella?"*

And he would say, "Borrow my umbrella, meisje? Of course, of course!"

But Mr. Mainz was not there. She could not ask him. Why not borrow it anyway? After all she would bring it right back, after lunch, only one hour from now.

Mr. Mainz won't mind . . . Mr. Mainz won't mind at all . . . he'll want me to use it . . . he probably keeps it here for anyone who needs it.

Suki lifted the umbrella from its brass hook.

Why, it was as light as a feather, and opened as easily as her locket, and the silver swan's head fit her hand as though it had been measured for her.

I can even walk through the door with this

umbrella raised, she thought. *A good thing too, because the rain is pounding on the cement steps outside.*

Even though it was noon, a couple of customers were in the Gosho Gift Shop when Suki arrived home. Her mother was talking to them, so Suki propped the red umbrella inside the door and flipped off her boots.

"Excuse me a moment," Mother said to the customers. "Your lunch is on the table, Suki. Daddy has gone to the Merchandise Mart, and I'm busy, so help yourself, dear."

"All right, Mother," Suki said, but she thought, *she does an awful lot of my thinking for me.*

Slowly Suki climbed the stairway to the apartment where she lived above the shop owned by her daddy. The kitchen was shiny clean, and on the table a place was set for her.

The peanut butter-plum jam sandwich didn't taste as good as usual, and Suki gulped the glass of milk. She didn't want that speckled banana Mother had placed beside her plate.

Best Friend had spoiled this perfectly keen rainy day by refusing to leave his perch in the shelter of the Paradise tree outside her window. But Suki decided she would speak to him anyway.

She walked down the long hall to her room. The rain had swollen the window frame, and she had to tug and lift with all of her might.

"Are you there, Best Friend?" she called.

There was no answer—just that cluck, cluck, cluck she did not like.

"Just because I'm glad it's raining, you don't have to be impolite," Suki said. "Stop that clucking and talk to me."

She had never spoken a cross word to the Invisible Peacock before. He huddled dejectedly under the branch with the thickest leaves. There seemed to be a great distance between them . . . a distance filled with the grayness and hissing of the rain, but he finally said, "I'm truly sorry, Suki. I don't feel well today. It hurts my throat to talk."

"Oh, that's too bad," Suki said. The tone of her voice was more disappointed than it was sympathetic. She hated for anyone to be sick. It was a lot of bother.

"Best Friend, I have lots to tell you, but I'll wait until tonight."

Without saying good-bye or I hope you'll feel better, without another word she closed the window.

Downstairs again, she put on her raincoat and went to the front door of the shop where she had left her boots and the red umbrella. The boots were there, but the umbrella was gone!

Suki thought she would smother with panic. *What if a customer had taken it by mistake? . . . more people had come in, to get out of the rain probably. . . . Mother wouldn't want to be interrupted while waiting on them . . . and she must not know about the umbrella anyway . . . but what can I do?*

"I put the umbrella in the bathtub, Suki," Mother said without turning around. "It was dripping all over the place."

Now how did she know I was looking for the umbrella? Suki thought quietly to herself.

25

"Where did you get it?" Mother asked. Still she didn't turn around. Suki was glad. That made it easier to say, "Oh, a friend loaned it to me."

Quickly she collected umbrella and boots and started back to the Louisa May Alcott School.

This time as she passed Riggs', the baker called, "Looks like she's set in for a spell, Suki."

I guess he means the rain is going to stay, Suki thought, and called back, "I hope so."

I hope it lasts and lasts, but if it does, Best Friend may never walk with me again . . . I do miss him . . . nothing is the same without him . . . I wonder what he'll say about the umbrella . . . what does one do with a sick peacock?

There's Butch. Maybe he'll know.

Butch saluted as Suki walked toward him. He even held the school door open and let her enter first. Two months ago he wouldn't have done that. He used to bully her and call her Slant Eyes and step on her clean sneakers. But that was before the accident—before the brick wall fell on him. He might have been buried alive if Suki hadn't rescued him. Now they were friends in spite of Butch being a grade ahead.

"Hurry up, Suki—it's really coming down!" Butch pulled the door closed with a bang.

Suki lowered the red umbrella and snapped it shut. It trailed a ribbon of water behind them as they went to the basement lockers.

"Butch, do you know how to cure a sick peacock? Best Friend isn't feeling well today."

"What a dumb question," Butch laughed. "Who in the world would know the answer to that one?"

Suki knew that Butch had his doubts about Best Friend, because he couldn't see him or talk to him the way she did. But he didn't make fun of her anymore for having an invisible friend.

27

"Best Friend says some peacocks die from getting wet."

Butch tried to look serious. "Don't worry, Suki. Invisible peacocks don't die."

As Butch slammed the door of his locker and took the stairs two at a time, Suki thought, *He talks to me as though I were a child.*

For the second time today, she hung up her raincoat and pulled off her boots. *Why don't I wait until tomorrow to take the umbrella back to Mr. Mainz? He won't mind if I take it home overnight, and maybe the rain will stop by morning.*

For a full minute she stood there trying to decide, then when she had completely convinced herself, she stood the umbrella in the corner of her locker, and closed the door softly.

This time she passed Mr. Mainz's office without looking in, because out of the corner of her eye she saw he was there. In fact, she hurried a little. His back was turned toward the door. He didn't see her. Funny how her heart beat hard and quick.

When I come back here after classes, I'll stop and talk to Mr. Mainz, Suki thought. *I'll say: "You weren't here at lunch time, and it was pouring rain, so I borrowed your umbrella, Mr. Mainz. I hope you don't mind." And he will say: "Anytime, little meisje—you may borrow it anytime you need it."*

He was sure to say that, so why was her heart pounding? No one would dream the umbrella did not belong to her. Butch hadn't asked her about it. And Mr. Mainz was having such a busy day he hadn't noticed it was missing. Besides, it must be very old. It leaked a little where the silver ribs had worn the silk from stretching. It was faded too. The light pricked through. No, Mr. Mainz wouldn't mind her using his old umbrella.

But the afternoon seemed endless; the class periods dragged tiresomely. The windows were down; it was stuffy. Usually Suki had fun at recess, but this day, this rainy day, no one could go outside.

Everyone went to the gym—to play games! She didn't want to play anything.

If only I could have a quiet talk with Best Friend instead of being in all this hubbub! These kids are screaming like Indians! And why doesn't that teacher stop blowing his whistle?

Finally, recess was over, and the classes lined up to go to the next period.

As they left the gym, there stood Mr. Mainz in the hall. He looked straight at Suki. She expected him to reach out and stop her when she passed. Instead, he smiled and said, "How is the little *meisje* with the dancing feet today?"

"Fine, Mr. Mainz." Suki smiled too.

He's just the same, she told herself. *He doesn't mind that I hung that old umbrella in my locker—not at all.*

She should have felt better after that, but she didn't.

When the last bell rang at 3:30, Suki jumped. She had waited and waited for it, but it surprised her. What a strange, mixed-up, sticky day it had been. Now she would have to take four books for homework, because she hadn't used the study period. And they would get all wet. She hated to get books or papers wet. *But then why should they get wet?*

That was the question that popped into her mind as she passed Mr. Mainz's office again. He wasn't there. The door with its sign— PRIVATE—was open. But Mr. Mainz wasn't there.

If he had been there, Suki was sure she would have gone in and said, "Mr. Mainz, I have all of this homework to do, and you know it's raining cats 'n dogs—may I please use your umbrella to keep my books from getting wet?"

He would look over the top of his glasses and nod and say: "Of course, little meisje with the dancing feet, you are welcome to use my umbrella—anytime!"

Since Suki was sure he would say that, she was soon on her way home, the red umbrella held jauntily over her head.

5

By 8:30 that Wednesday night, the rain had turned to mist—a mist so fine it seemed to collect into rings of color around the street lights and drift in ghostly clouds across the yard behind the Gosho Gift Shop.

From her window, Suki could not see the high back fence nor the squatty little pine tree. The white gravel path melted into an eerie blur, and when Suki leaned out the window, feathery mist tickled her nose and tongue and hands and arms. *Surely Best Friend would not mind the mist,* she thought.

"Good evening, Suki."

"Oh, Best Friend, am I ever glad you're here! Are you feeling any better?"

"Yes, my dear—the moment the rain slackened my health began improving."

Then the Invisible Peacock stretched his long snake-like neck from under the tent of green leaves which had sheltered him.

"Have you eaten?" Suki asked.

"Yes, Suki, worms have been plentiful, and I must say, they go down easily."

"Worms don't scratch a sore throat the way corn and gravel do, do they?"

"Mercifully, no."

"Another important thing is your having a warm place to sleep, Best Friend. So you must come in here with me for the night."

When the Invisible Peacock hesitated, Suki said, "Don't you want to come in with me? Haven't you missed me today? I've missed you. And this way we can make up for lost time."

As Best Friend stepped from the branch of the beautiful Paradise tree to the window sill, a foghorn groaned somewhere on the great lake.

"You are generous to share your room with me, Suki," he said once he was inside. "This will be the first time I've had a roof over my head since leaving the zoo."

Suki lowered the window to shut out the damp.

"Now, just make yourself at home," she said, climbing into bed. She had helped with the supper dishes, hurried through her homework, undressed, brushed her teeth, brushed her hair, and said her prayers—all in one hour flat!

"It even smells dry in here," said the Peacock. "Can it be . . . is there a faint fragrance of jasmine?"

"Oh, that's the new bath powder Grandmother sent to me from California." Suki arranged the fat pillows against the headboard of the bed and fell back into them sighing. "Whew-ee! What a day!" She turned off the light beside her. "Let's talk in the dark, Best Friend. Want to?"

"Yes, let's talk in the dark," said the Peacock. "Of course, this room is strange to me, which makes me a little restless, so don't mind if I wander around until I find a perching place."

"Can you see in the dark the way they say cats do?" Suki asked.

"No, Suki, peacocks don't see well at night. But we do have one thing in common with cats."

"What?"

"They predict the weather as do we. Listen to this old Italian saying."

If a cat washes her face o'er the ear,
'tis a sign that
the weather'll be fine and clear.

"In Holland they had another prediction."

It will rain if cats sit
with their backs to the fire.

Suki giggled and giggled. "Go on, Best Friend— please, please tell me some more."

"Well, do you know this one?"

A fly on your nose;
You slap it, and it goes;
If it comes back again
It will bring a good rain.

Suki clapped her hands. "More! Tell me more!"
"Let me see," said the Peacock. "How about a rain song?"

It's raining,
It's pouring,
The old man is snoring.
Bumped his head,
As he went to bed,
And he couldn't get up in the morning.
Rain—rain—go away—
Come again some other day.

Suki sang the last line over and over until she remembered: *But I don't want the rain to go away!* Suddenly there was a

S-W-O-O-S-H-C-L-A-T-T-E-R-K-A-L-U-M-P.

"What was that?" whispered the Peacock in alarm.
Suki snapped on the light. "Oh, you know—probably it was only that old umbrella."

"Umbrella? Had I known you had an umbrella, I would have walked to school with you today, Suki."

"Well, if it's still raining you can walk with me tomorrow. That's why I brought it home."

"It is a most extraordinary umbrella," said the Peacock, peering closely at the silver handle. "Shouldn't you open it up to dry?"

Suki bounced out of bed and raised the red umbrella. She held it over her head and looked at herself in the mirror.

"Everyone should have an umbrella, don't you think, Best Friend? One never knows when it might rain."

"*Exactly*," said the Peacock. It was the first time he had used his favorite word in two days—a sure sign he was feeling better. "I certainly think umbrellas are underrated these days, Suki."

She knew they were about to have a good talk so she placed the umbrella in a corner and got back into bed. "You really don't see very many," Suki said.

"No, the ladies wear these homely plastic things that tie under their chins, and the men go bareheaded. No wonder most everyone has sinus trouble." The Invisible Peacock coughed.

"Who, do you suppose, made up such a funny word—umbrella?"

"I don't know, Suki. But our English word comes from a Latin word which means *little shadow*."

"Oh, I like that," Suki said. "You are the wisest creature in all the world, Best Friend. You know all about everything!"

"Not everything," the Invisible Peacock said. "There will always be much to learn. As I told you when we met the first time, I am wise, because I am old."

For a moment or two it was silent in the room. Then Suki said, "You probably know the umbrella is not mine."

"I only know I haven't seen it before, Suki. Whose is it?"

Suki looked out the window. "It belongs to Mr. Mainz. He's the janitor at school."

"The man who smiles at you and calls you the little *meisje* with the dancing feet?"

"Yes, he's the one."

"It's quite valuable I would guess," said the Peacock. "He must be a nice man to let you use it."

Suki frowned. "He didn't let me use it, exactly."

She wished the Invisible Peacock would say something instead of waiting for her to go on, but he didn't.

"If you're thinking I stole that old umbrella, I didn't!"

"I had no such thought, I assure you," said Best Friend. "But you sound as though you're trying to convince yourself. How do you happen to have Mr. Mainz's umbrella?"

Suki shifted the pillows. "I didn't steal it. I borrowed it."

"Without telling Mr. Mainz?"

"Well, I would have told him, but he wasn't in his office right then."

"Couldn't you have left a note, Suki?"

"I didn't think of that. Honest, I didn't."

Suki knew that Best Friend believed her. *But would Mr. Mainz? What if Mr. Mainz thought she had stolen the umbrella? He might tell her teachers and Mother and Daddy and Butch. That would be horrible. She would have to run away. No one wanted a thief around.*

"But I'm not a thief," she said aloud. "No matter what Mr. Mainz thinks, I'm not a thief. I plan to take the umbrella back—tomorrow morning—first thing—I borrowed it, that's all."

She couldn't believe that a few hours ago she had been proud to walk home in the rain with the red umbrella protecting her. Now she wished she had never seen it nor felt the curve in the swan's neck. It was like a shadow all right. A shadow so dark she could feel it heavy on her chest. *How could that old umbrella make her want to cry?*

"I'm sure Mr. Mainz will take your word for it, Suki," the Peacock said. "If you tell him you intended to borrow the umbrella overnight and not keep it, he will believe you. But, of course, if he's like most people he won't appreciate your having borrowed it without asking his permission."

There was kindness in Best Friend's tone of voice even if he was being very, very serious. "Remember the other day when Butch ran off with your model glider? He hadn't stolen it, had he?"

"No, he brought it back, but he broke it."

41

"Yes, Suki, he broke it, and he didn't think that mattered much, because he said he could make you another one just like it."

"But he couldn't, Best Friend. Daddy made that one."

"Exactly. *That* glider can never be replaced, because of what it means to you—only to you. To Butch it is no different from the dozen he has made. And he'll replace it, but it won't be the same, will it, Suki?"

"No. Daddy made that one, and he let me glue the tail."

"So, you see, owning something can be important for reasons only the owner understands. That's one big reason you and I must respect the property of others."

"I haven't broken the umbrella, though."

"No, Suki, but what if someone had picked it up in the

shop, or the wind had blown it wrongside-out? Sometimes when we borrow, we borrow trouble."

"That would have been trouble all right," Suki said, thinking back to those suspense-filled minutes at noon when her mother had moved the umbrella without her knowing. "I'll take it back to Mr. Mainz in the morning, before school begins."

Best Friend smiled. "And I'll go with you."

6

The clock with its blue frame and bright face and gay tick-tick told Suki it was 8:30 as she tiptoed through the Gosho Gift Shop. It was 8:30 Thursday morning. She hoped Mother and Daddy would go on talking about the weather and not notice that she was leaving for school earlier than usual.

"I thought the rain was over when we went to bed last night," Mother said. "Now, look at it."

"The paper says it will clear this afternoon," Daddy said turning to the sports section of the *Tribune*.

"Well, it can't stop soon enough to suit me." Mother was unpacking a crate of wind chimes. "The shop is as musty as a dungeon."

From the front door, Suki called, "Bye!" but she
called softly. If only that little bell on the door would
forget to ring. Mother and Daddy didn't notice really
even though Mother waved.

Suki raised the umbrella and said, "Stay close to
me, Best Friend. This old umbrella isn't very large as
you can see."

*It takes less than ten minutes to walk to school if I
don't play on the way,* Suki thought. *Mr. Mainz is sure
to be in his office now.* She put her raincoat and boots
in the locker just as she had done yesterday.

"I'll be back at noon, Best Friend. Wait for me right here."

"All right," said the Invisible Peacock. "I know Mr. Mainz will understand about the umbrella if you tell him the truth."

Why wouldn't I tell him the truth? Suki thought as she hurried down the hall.

There was Mr. Mainz's office, and the door was open. All of a sudden her feet felt as though they were weighted with lead.

By the time she took the last four steps to the door she was tired enough to fall in a heap. Then she looked inside the tiny room. There was the rolltop

desk closed up tight, the chair in its place, the shelves dusted and tidy, the wastepaper barrels empty, and the hall tree waiting.

He isn't here. Suki told herself. *I don't need to tell him anything. I can just hang the umbrella on the hook. Mr. Mainz may not have missed it. If he hasn't, there's no point in telling him I've had it. No one will know that. The important thing is to put it back. That's the important thing.*

Suki hung the red umbrella on the brass hook from which she had taken it.

Outside her homeroom, Suki saw a group of boys and girls reading something on the bulletin

board. Butch was there, and when he saw her coming, he yelled, "Hey, Suki, guess what?"

"What?"

"Old Man Mainz's umbrella is missing."

Suki almost said, "No, it isn't." But she caught herself.

"Miss Kelly has a notice on the board," Butch turned around to read the words to Suki. *She could read just as well as he could. Oh, well, let him act like a know-it-all.*

Butch imitated Miss Kelly's voice as he read:

Lost

Will the person who took the umbrella from the janitor's office please return it? No questions will be asked, but it must be returned at once.

(Signed) Miss Kelly
Room 203

and everyone laughed. Everyone but Suki.

48

"I told you somebody would swipe something out of Old Man Mainz's cubbyhole if he left the door open," Butch said.

"Do you have to call him *Old Man Mainz?* He's so nice."

"What's that got to do with his age, Suki? He *is* old—as old as George Washington," Butch said, then he poked her with his armload of books in a friendly way. "Say, what's eating you, Suki? The rain getting you down?"

"Wouldn't you like to know?" Suki asked and went to her homeroom desk.

The tardy bell rang. Everyone sat down. Miss Kelly took the attendance. "Will you come here, please, Suki?" she said.

Suki always liked to help Miss Kelly, but she wished she had called on someone else today.

"These pictures have been graded," the teacher said, handing a stack of drawings to Suki. "Pass them out for me, please."

"Yes, Miss Kelly."

"Thank you, Suki."

Up and down the rows of desks Suki went reading the names of her classmates: *Beth, Vivian, Paul, Maria, Kevin, Toy, Roxanne, Scott, Iris, Claudette, Randy, Mary Kay, George, Eugene, Daphne, Edward, Riva, Werner, Alfredo, Judy* (Judy Matsuoka from her Sunday school class), *Denise, and Ken.*

Her own drawing made twenty-three. She kept it on the bottom of the stack while passing out the others. As Suki sat down at her desk again, she looked at it. She had forgotten the picture. There was the shell with the red umbrella floating above it.

Miss Kelly knew about the umbrella!

7

By noon Suki had made up her mind. If Mr. Mainz was in his office, she was going to go right in and tell him what had happened.

She was tired of this mixed-up feeling; the shadow of the umbrella seemed to darken everything. Best Friend would be waiting, and although she had planned to let him think she had talked to Mr. Mainz when she really hadn't, now she knew the only thing she could do was to be truthful.

She would tell Mr. Mainz everything, and maybe it would turn out all right, the way Best Friend had said it would. He had said, "I know Mr. Mainz will understand about the umbrella if you tell him the truth."

Suki walked down the steps, thinking, thinking.
The door was open.
He was there.
"Hello . . . hello! How is the little *meisje* with
the dancing feet?" Mr. Mainz called.
He may never say that again after I tell him, Suki

thought. "Hello, Mr. Mainz. May I have a talk with you?" Her voice was shaky.

Mr. Mainz peered over the top of his glasses curiously and nodded. "Of course, little *meisje*, of course. Come in."

Suki wanted to turn and run, but it was too late.

"This is a private talk, Mr. Mainz. There is something I have to tell you."

Mr. Mainz pulled out the chair and motioned for Suki to sit down. "Now, we can talk."

"You sit in the chair, Mr. Mainz," Suki said. "I'd rather stand up." The old janitor sat down facing her. His eyes were level with hers. They could look at each other.

"Mr. Mainz—I took your umbrella."

"Did you, little *meisje*? That's funny—it must have found its way back. See? It hangs in the accustomed place."

"But I put it back," Suki said. "Even before I saw Miss Kelly's notice on the bulletin board."

Mr. Mainz rubbed his chin. "I told Miss Kelly not to bother—my umbrella would come back when it got ready."

"Miss Kelly knows I had it, but she thinks I stole it. I didn't, Mr. Mainz—I didn't steal your umbrella. I borrowed it. And not just to keep out of the rain either. My raincoat has a hood. But I thought it was so beautiful and wanted to look at it for a while."

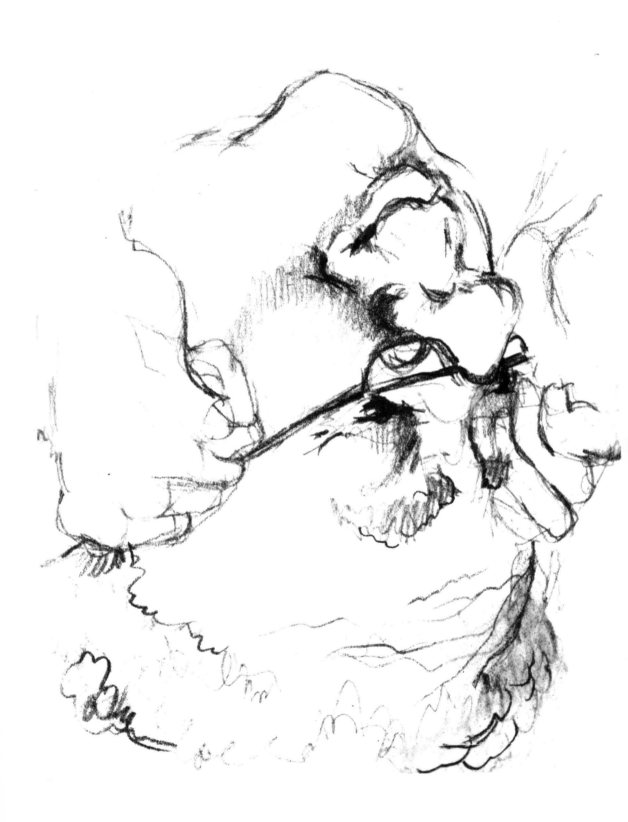

"I understand, little *meisje*." Mr. Mainz reached for the umbrella and lifted it from the hook. "Yes, beautiful it is. And you are beautiful—as was the child for whom it was made a long, long time ago. Her home was far from here in a city strange to you—Amsterdam, Holland. Her father was an artisan. All over Europe, the old country, he was known for his work in silver. For his only daughter, he had this little umbrella made. And he, himself, fashioned the silver handle to fit her hand."

Mr. Mainz traced the fine engraving of the swan's head with a stiff finger—its joints were swollen and red—but there was something so gentle in the touch that matched the feeling in his eyes and voice.

"Here, little *meisje*, you hold it." He placed the umbrella handle in her right hand then closed her fingers around it. "Ahh, it fits you too!"

"It *is* old, very old, isn't it, Mr. Mainz?" Suki asked.

"Yes, little *meisje*. See here, inside the curve of the handle: *for Eda—Amsterdam—1909*." Mr. Mainz sighed, "You know that 1909 was a long, long time ago. I was your age then, and Eda was six. She and her parents lived near my family. On Raphael Plein it was. We took picnics to the park, and always the umbrella went along. My legs grew fast, and I would have to duck down to look at Eda under the umbrella. She would laugh and toss her long black hair. Her eyes were black and laughing.

The red umbrella was a part of the way she looked then."

"She was your favorite playmate?" asked Suki.

57

"Always, little *meisje*, for when we grew up, I became her husband. Twenty-three years she was my heart, my dearest treasure."

Mr. Mainz took off his glasses and rubbed his eyes with the back of his hand. Suki could tell he was sad.

"Did something happen to her—to Eda?"

Mr. Mainz closed his eyes, and the silence between them was solemn. Finally, he said, "She was killed. She was killed by a madman. A man named Adolph Hitler. He tried to kill all of us—Jews. But I remain. Sometimes I wish I were with Eda."

Suki laid the umbrella on Mr. Mainz's knees and put her small hands over his large ones.

"I'm sorry, Mr. Mainz. I'm sorry about your Eda. And I *am* sorry about the umbrella. I didn't know it was your very favorite thing. I had no right to borrow it. My best friend says owning something can be important for reasons only the owner understands. That's the reason I must respect the property of others."

Mr. Mainz put on his glasses and looked at Suki over the top of them the way he always had.

"Property is things, little *meisje*," he said. "Things do not last. They are not forever. But they are often symbols, or signs, of memories and experiences that hate and war and death cannot kill. The way a lion is a sign of courage in your storybooks, this umbrella is a sign of love and happiness to me. But you are

the only one to know. God made each one of us with a deep private place inside. This we must also respect, little *meisje*. You and God know what this old umbrella means to me, and *why*. But you will not share the *why* with any other person. This is my private memory."

"Thank you, Mr. Mainz."

That was all Suki could say. She meant so much more, but all she could say was, "Thank you, Mr. Mainz."

She took the umbrella over to the hall tree and hung it on the brass hook.

"I'll never borrow again without asking," she said.

Mr. Mainz got slowly to his feet. "Anytime, little *meisje* with the dancing feet," he said. "Anytime you can ask, and you know what I will say?"

"Yes, Mr. Mainz, I know," Suki said.

8

Best Friend would be waiting at the lockers. Suki was sure of that. But she felt almost closer to Mr. Mainz. She could *see* him. She could hold his hand. She needed Mr. Mainz for her friend too, the same as she needed the Invisible Peacock.

We need to know some things by seeing, she thought. *They help us to be sure of important things we can't see.*

Miss Kelly can't know about me inside right now, because she can only see the outside of me. She still thinks I stole the umbrella, probably. And if she thinks that, she thinks I have a heavy, bad feeling inside. But I don't. Everything inside is fixed. The shadow has gone away.

Just the same, I feel Mr. Mainz's sadness.

"Oh, there you are, Best Friend," Suki said, opening the locker door. "We're going to be awfully late for lunch." She pulled on her raincoat.

"You won't need that, Suki," said the Invisible Peacock. "It's clearing off. The sun is coming out. The rain has ended."

Side by side, they walked as fast as they could to the corner, and while they waited for the Safety Patrol boy to take them across Clark Street, Best Friend asked, "Did Mr. Mainz understand, Suki?"

"Oh, yes, exactly the way you said he would. And I told him the truth the way you told me to."

"I'm proud of you, Suki. Truly proud!"

The Invisible Peacock pranced ahead, then turned around to face her. As he did, he shook himself and unfurled his train until the coppery feathers with their blue-green eyes arced into a shimmering fan. In the sunlight his topknot and his vest of blue glistened with the luster of emerald and sapphire jewels.

The beauty of it made Suki think of Mr. Mainz. She wished he could see it too.

Joyce Blackburn has written fifteen published books since leaving a professional career in Chicago radio. Her recording of *Suki and the Invisible Peacock* led to a contract for her first book of the same title. Subsequent prize-winning titles for young readers have made Blackburn well-known among librarians and teachers. She has also gained recognition in the field of popular historical biography and enjoys an enthusiastic adult following. Blackburn, a resident of St. Simons Island, Georgia, received the 1996 Governor's Award in the humanities from the Georgia Humanities Council. Her works are in the Special Collections of the Woodruff Library at Emory University, Atlanta, Georgia.